Snowshoe the Hare

KATHRYN WHITE   RUTH RIVERS

Go Bananas

For Ma, with love
K.W.

For Diego and Gabriella
R.R.

EGMONT
We bring stories to life

First published in Great Britain 2005
by Egmont Books Limited
239 Kensington High Street
London W8 6SA
Text copyright © Kathryn White 2005
Illustrations copyright © Ruth Rivers 2005
The author and illustrator have asserted their moral rights
Paperback ISBN 1 4052 1765 0
1 3 5 7 9 10 8 6 4 2
A CIP catalogue record for this title is available from the British Library
Printed and bound in Singapore

Contents

Go Bananas

Melting!

Snowshoe the Arctic hare sniffed the autumn air outside his nest to smell if Grizzly was lurking nearby.

Something rustled in a bush so Snowshoe hid his speckled, brown body out of sight.

'Gotcha!' Suddenly, Snowshoe's friend Red Squirrel leapt out at him.

'You wait!' shouted Snowshoe, chasing Squirrel.

I'll get you!

Aagh!

Just then, brown Lemming
scurried out from under a bush.
He was muttering busily to himself
and didn't notice Snowshoe and Squirrel
zooming towards him.

'Look out!' cried Squirrel,
grinding to a halt.

But it was too late.

Snowshoe couldn't stop himself and crashed straight into Squirrel with a mighty clunk. Squirrel and Snowshoe rolled into a furry ball and tumbled past Lemming, down the hillside, landing with a splash at the water's edge.

Oof!

'A giant furball out of control?' thought Lemming. 'Run for cover!' he cried and scampered off.

Snowshoe and Squirrel stood up and shook the cold water from their fur.

'Brrr!' said Snowshoe with a shiver.

Shh!

'Be quiet, you two,' said Otter angrily,
popping his head out of the water. 'How am
I going to catch fish with you making such
a racket?'

Silver fish darted in all directions
from the water's edge.

'We're only playing,' said
Squirrel, suddenly diving
at Snowshoe.

'Winter's coming and you're playing? Well, who will you play with when Snowshoe turns white and melts with the snow?' Otter asked.

'Melt with the snow?' said Snowshoe, trembling at the thought of melting.

'Yes, melt. You are a brown hare now but each day, as winter gets closer, you'll turn whiter and whiter. Then in spring when the hot sun shines down you'll melt away. Just like the snow does,' Otter said.

Melt?

Snowshoe was horrified.

Squirrel looked at all the other animals rushing around, busily building up their food stores in preparation for the coming winter. 'Snowshoe won't melt. He will burrow and hibernate, won't you?' said Squirrel.

'But I don't know how to burrow or hibernate. I live in a nest,' said Snowshoe.

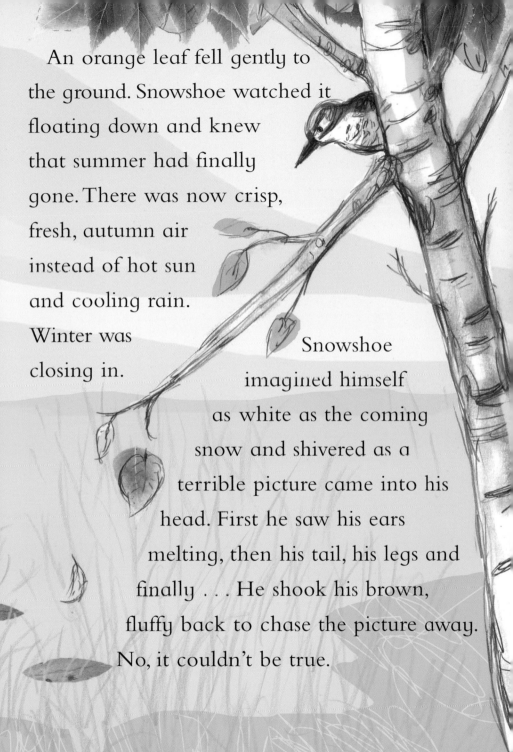

An orange leaf fell gently to the ground. Snowshoe watched it floating down and knew that summer had finally gone. There was now crisp, fresh, autumn air instead of hot sun and cooling rain. Winter was closing in.

Snowshoe imagined himself as white as the coming snow and shivered as a terrible picture came into his head. First he saw his ears melting, then his tail, his legs and finally . . . He shook his brown, fluffy back to chase the picture away. No, it couldn't be true.

Otter snorted. 'Snowshoe is a hare. Hare is Hare and Porcupine is Porcupine.'

'Did somebody mention my name?' said Porcupine.

They turned to see a small, prickly ball waddling slowly up to them.

Porcupine looked at the group, puzzled, but then Porcupine always looked puzzled. 'What's the matter?' he asked.

'Snowshoe's going to melt,' Squirrel said anxiously.

'Really?' said Porcupine, surprised. 'When?'

'I'm going to turn white and then disappear with the snow in the spring,' cried Snowshoe. 'Otter told me.'

Otter puffed his chest out importantly.

'Now that you come to mention it, I remember a hare who turned white and disappeared in the last spring thaw,' Porcupine said, looking up at the sky and imagining melting hares.

Hmm...

'What bit melted first?' Squirrel asked, concerned.

'I can't remember,' Porcupine said vaguely. 'But when the weather gets warmer in the spring, the heat causes snow and ice to melt to water.'

Snowshoe's fur prickled up on his back as he looked at the bright sun. 'I'm going to melt into water,' he thought. His tummy felt funny, as if it was full of butterflies.

'Quite right,' said Otter
self–importantly.
'Sunshine, plus warmer
weather and Bob's
your uncle!'

'I have an Uncle Bob!'
exclaimed Porcupine.

Otter frowned and
everyone looked at each
other in confusion.

'What am I going to
do?' asked Snowshoe.

A Place to Hide

'If you hide from the sun perhaps you won't melt,' suggested Squirrel.

'Mmmmm, worth a try,' Otter said, twitching his whiskers, unimpressed.

They all looked around for somewhere for Snowshoe to hide but the autumn sun shone down into all the nooks and crannies.

Even Otter's cold river suddenly
looked bright and warm.

19

'You can hide in my tree-house,' said Squirrel, trying to picture squeezing a big hare like Snowshoe into his tiny little nest. 'Thank you but I can't climb trees and anyway, it's warm in your cosy nest,' Snowshoe replied sadly. What was he going to do?

He's too **big!**

Whooper the swan drifted serenely up to the water's edge. 'What is the matter?' she asked haughtily.

'I'm worried because I'm going to turn white and . . .' But before Snowshoe could finish, Whooper hissed, 'What's wrong with being white?' Offended, she ruffled her soft white feathers.

Squirrel

'He'll disappear with the snow when it melts,' Porcupine said, suddenly knowledgeable on the subject of melting hares.

'Oh dear,' Whooper exclaimed. 'I can fly off to warmer countries in the winter.' She raised her beak upwards and watched the flocks of birds migrating overhead. 'Then I fly back here in spring when it's nice and warm.'

Snowshoe trembled at the words 'spring' and 'warm'.

Just then brown Lemming
came charging past.

'Lemming, stop!' called Squirrel. 'Snowshoe
needs your advice.'

'Sorry, can't stop,' Lemming said urgently,
'and I wouldn't stand around here gossiping
if I were you. There's a giant ball of fur on
the loose and it nearly knocked me right off
my feet!' Lemming looked nervously around
then shot off again.

Quick!

'Don't worry, Snowshoe, we'll think of something,' said Squirrel. 'Listen, everyone. Snowshoe needs our help. Put on your thinking caps for a plan to prevent Snowshoe from melting in the spring.'

'I haven't got a thinking cap,' Porcupine said. 'I've always wanted one. Blue and woolly with white spots and a floppy bobble on the end.'

'It's not a real cap,' said the animals.

'Oh. Well, it would have stuck to my spikes anyway.' Porcupine prickled in disappointment.

'We'll meet again soon with a plan to help Snowshoe,' said Squirrel, racing off.

The Plan

Every day Snowshoe sniffed nervously
from his nest, waiting for the first fall of
snow but it didn't come. The weather
was changing though. The sky was
often grey and overcast and most
mornings the ground felt crisp
and hard and it sparkled
magically with frost.
It was getting
colder too.

Then one day when Squirrel and
Snowshoe were playing hide and seek
Squirrel gasped,
'Snowshoe, your legs
are turning as
white as snow.'

Oh, no!

Snowshoe looked down in
horror. 'It's happening!' he
shrieked. 'I'm going to
melt, I'm going
to melt!'

He darted around the field
in great circles.

Help!

Squirrel called an urgent meeting
of all the animals to the riverside.

When everyone saw Snowshoe, they
noticed that not only were his legs
turning white, but he also had flecks of
fluffy white fur all over his back.

Otter popped his nose up from
the river and stared at Snowshoe's
new white legs. 'Oh dear,' he
said in a worried way, over
and over again.
'It's started.'

I'm turning white!

Porcupine arrived, proudly displaying a cardboard box he'd stuck on to his prickles. 'Look what I've found. Snowshoe can hide from the sun in here,' he said helpfully.

'Rubbish,' sniffed Otter. 'He won't be able to see where he's going and anyway *I* have a better plan.'

'Is it sun-proof?' Porcupine demanded huffily.

'Sun-proof and Porcupine-proof,' Otter announced snobbily.

'Tell us quickly,' everyone said, gathering round Otter.

'Snowshoe has started to turn white and will soon melt with the snow but . . . when it snows again next year, we'll re-make him out of fresh snow.'

First all the animals looked puzzled, then amazed, then chuckled in disbelief.

'It's better than Porcupine's box,' Otter said quickly.

'Not much,' Squirrel replied.

'I'll make Snowshoe's feet,' Whooper whooped.

'I'll do his ears,' Porcupine said, inspired. 'What if we forget what he looks like and make him back to front, upside down or even worse, looking like Grizzly or Wolverine?' said Woodpecker from her hole in the tree.

We don't want another Wolverine, thought Porcupine in horror. At least Grizzly hibernates for the winter but Wolverine stays awake and hunts all year long.

Squirrel rubbed his nose
thoughtfully, then picked up a
long twig. 'Let's draw a picture
in the mud of how we will put
Snowshoe back together again.'
'Oh no,' thought Snowshoe.
'Next spring I might end up
looking scary like Grizzly
and no one will want
to play with me.'
Squirrel carefully
drew Snowshoe's head.

I'll start.

Everyone thought it was a good head.

Snowshoe gave a little sigh of relief. But suddenly Porcupine snatched the twig from Squirrel and drew ridiculously long, wonky ears.

Snowshoe quivered as he watched the strange picture of himself growing in the mud.

'My turn,' said Woodpecker, sweeping down and around in a circle as she drew Snowshoe's tail.

Bit by bit, everyone added to the picture of Snowshoe.

33

As Snowshoe watched them drawing, he became dizzier and dizzier at the sight of the monster in the mud until he toppled backwards in a hopeless, muddy heap. 'That doesn't look like me. It looks like Grizzly!' Snowshoe cried out in alarm.

Everyone looked at the finished picture.

'YUCK!' Whooper exclaimed.

'Disaster!' said Squirrel.

'Horrendous!' said Otter.

'Awful!' cried Porcupine.

'You'll never be able to put me back the way I really was, am . . . should be,' said Snowshoe. 'Oh, help!'

Porcupine held up the cardboard box, and everyone sighed.

Mr Collared Lemming to You

'What's the problem?' said a friendly voice.

A mysterious animal stepped out of the shadows. It was as white as a snowball and it stood looking intently at them all. It was strangely familiar.

The group stepped back nervously.

Porcupine hid under his box.

'Uh hum, do we know you?' Otter asked timidly, plopping back down into the water.

36

'Of course you know me! I'm Lemming,' said Lemming, feeling quite insulted. 'Mr Collared Lemming to you,' he said formally to Otter.

'You can't be Lemming. Lemming is brown. You're white,' said Squirrel.

Whooper looked in disbelief at Lemming's beautiful white fur. 'It can't be Lemming. Impossible,' she snorted jealously.

Lemming walked up to them and smiled. 'Look closely,' he said.

It's me!

All the animals stepped closer and studied the stranger.

'Well, don't take all day. There's a dangerous fur ball flying about in these parts,' said Lemming.

They gasped in amazement.

'It *is* Lemming!' Squirrel exclaimed. 'It's definitely our friend Lemming.'

'I don't believe it!' exclaimed Porcupine. 'Is it really you, Lemming?'

I've got my winter coat on.

Lemming chuckled. 'Of course it's me, Porcupine,' he said, grooming his snowy fur.

'But what's happened to you? Why are you white?' said Snowshoe.

'Naturally I'm white. The snow's coming so I have a new white coat. Now I will blend in and won't be seen. Where are you all going to hide when Wolverine comes searching for food?' asked Lemming wisely.

Porcupine dived back under the old box.

'I'm turning white too, but Otter says I'm going to melt with the snow in spring,' Snowshoe said sadly.

'Melt? Melt?' Lemming shrieked with laughter. He laughed so much that he doubled over and fell with a plop in the mud.

'What a ridiculous idea! Melt?' Lemming hooted at Otter in disbelief.

'I . . . I've seen it with my own eyes. Hares turning white and disappearing with the snow,' said Otter, looking very uncomfortable.

'No, no, no,' Lemming laughed. 'Snowshoe's growing his smart winter coat to hide him from Grizzly and Wolverine. It's camouflage, like mine.'

'So I won't melt when spring comes then?' asked Snowshoe breathlessly.

'Of course not! In spring, you'll change back into your smart brown, speckled coat so that you won't be spotted in the bushes by predators,' said Lemming. Snowshoe was delighted! 'I'm not going to melt after all! Whoopee!' he shouted, hopping around his friends and kicking up the leaves with joy. 'I can't wait for summer to come back, we'll have great fun!'

Hooray!

Everyone laughed.

Lemming looked at Otter. 'Special animals adapt and change colour with the seasons,' he said.

Snowshoe puffed up with pride.

'I knew that all along,' said Otter, blushing and twitching his whiskers.

Everyone looked at Otter and laughed as the first snowflake of the year landed right on the end of his nose.

This is the Earth. Different parts of the Earth have different climates because they get different amounts of heat from the sun. Places near the equator are hot, and places near the North and South Poles are cold.

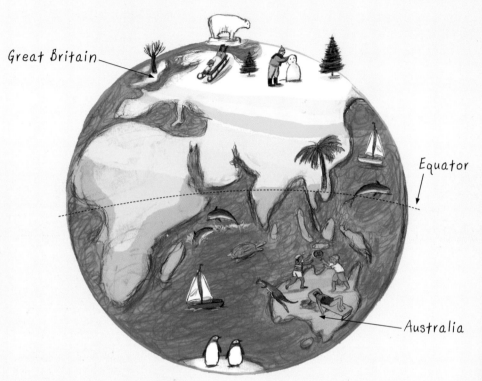

Great Britain

Equator

Australia

Animals adapt to the weather and the season. Snowshoe turns white in winter to blend in with the snow. Some birds fly south to warmer lands in the winter.

The seasons change as the Earth moves round the sun each year. When it is winter north of the equator, in Great Britain for instance, it is summer in Australia.

Cats and dogs grow thicker fur coats in the winter and moult (drop hairs) in the spring when it gets warmer.

The Arctic (North Pole) has a polar climate. It is very cold there! The Arctic is an ocean covered with a sheet of ice, with land surrounding it.

I live in the Arctic.

The Antarctic (South Pole) is land covered with ice. It is even colder than the Arctic. Sometimes the ice breaks off to form icebergs. Icebergs are huge floating blocks of ice.

Both Poles have snow as well as ice. Snow is made when rain freezes into ice very high up in the air. Snowflakes are very beautiful and each snowflake has a different pattern.

Some mountains have snow. You can go skiing or snowboarding down lots of mountains. What else can you do in the snow?

In snowy places there are sometimes blizzards. Blizzards are snowstorms. They happen when the wind blows loose snow around very fast. They are dangerous because they are very cold and they make it difficult to see.

Did you know? The Arctic and the Antarctic are both deserts, even though they are cold.

What is the weather like today? Is the sun shining? Make a chart of the weather where you live for a week. It could look like this:

Monday	
Tuesday	
Wednesday	
Thursday	
Friday	
Saturday	
Sunday	

Does it change a lot? What do you think it would be like if you lived in the Arctic, like Snowshoe?

Making a Snowglobe

You will need
A clean, wide plastic jar or pot with a lid
White plasticine
A small figure
White glitter
A grown-up to help!

How to make it

1. Roll the plasticine into a pancake shape and press it into the bottom of the jar, so it looks like a snowy landscape. Make sure it is firmly stuck.

2. Press your figure into the plasticine and make sure it is secure.

3. Fill the jar with cold water to within 1cm of the top. Ask a grown-up to sprinkle 1 tablespoon (25 ml) of glitter into the water.

4. Ask a grown-up to screw the lid on tightly. Turn the jar upside down and shake gently.

Enjoy your very own snowglobe!

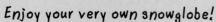